THE ROAD OF LIFE

OLGA MAE PASMORE

minna PRESS

ISBN 978-976-95693-6-2

A catalogue record of this book is available from the
National Library of Jamaica.

Ordering Information
Quantity (Bulk) Sales: Special discounts are available on quantity (bulk)
purchases by corporations, associations, and others.
For details, contact the publisher: sales@minnapress.com

Executive Editor: Lena J. Rose
Editor: Kimiko Kong
Designer: Mark Steven Weinberger

Published in Kingston Jamaica
by Minna Press, 204 Mountain View Avenue, Kingston 6, Jamaica

Dedication page photograph: *Innocence*, by Olga M. Pasmore
                        First Place Prize; Photographic Exhibition, 1959
                        The National Arena, Kingston, Jamaica

DEDICATION

This book is published posthumously and dedicated to
Olga Mae's grandchildren

Jean Alain

Natasha

Simone

Chad

Justin

Kyle

CONTENTS

Acknowledgement 6

Foreword 7

Preface 9

Songs of Childhood 12

My Town 13

The Blind Boy 15

Old Lady Picking Buttercups 16

And Forsaking All Others 17

The Morning Star at the Cursillo 22

Our Nation 23

The Clock Tower 24

Golden Days 25

Mist on the Purple Mountains 26

Deep In My Hills 37

A Gentle Kiss 40

Soft Moments 40

CONTENTS

The Leader of the Band   41

Drums of Calabar   42

Flamboyant   43

For My Friend Elsie   50

A Tribute to McArthur Ireland   51

La Chaumiere   52

Rosie   53

Mr. Gilou   62

The Leader of the Gang   63

A String of Fish   71

Martin Luther King   87

Rt. Hon. Norman Manley Q.C   88

The Road to Emmaus   89

The Road of Life   91

Olga Mae   92

ACKNOWLEDGEMENT

I must thank Mrs. Marcia McFarlane and Mrs. Anne Rae for working on this manuscript.

Also, Calvin Bowen for reading and making suggestions as well as writing the foreword.

FOREWORD

Olga Pasmore has left a legacy of literary gifts for her friends and admirers to enjoy. In her poems and her short stories runs a thread of love of life, of oneness with nature; and a deep and strong faith.

Hers was a quiet talent—one that did not shout from the housetops but which made a powerful impact on those who were privileged to be members of her inner circle and to read her writings.

Although basically a city person, she had the poet's love for the countryside—for the calm beauty of the rivers, the majesty of the trees, the wonder and magic of nature.

In her quiet unostentatious way, she was a true patriot, loving her native land with unwavering ardour, sharing in its triumphs and disasters.

This collection of her works reflects some of these aspects of her exemplary life as a talented daughter of Jamaica.

—Calvin Bowen

OLGA MAE PASMORE

1920-1989

PREFACE

This book of poems and short stories was my mother's life dream.

I was handed the contents of this book a year after my mother's death by my aunt and asked to look about it. One year later I finally opened the package and went through its contents.

My mother's death was not easy to deal with, added to the fact that these poems and short stories would bring back a lot of memories.

I have endeavoured to rise above the sad memories and reproduce; firstly her prize winning photograph on the front cover "Innocence" and her poems and short stories, several of them portray her patriotic spirit and that she was proud to be Jamaican.

Olga Mae Facey was born 25th May, 1920 to Ellen Hazel Peat and Aubrey Garfield Facey. She grew up on her father's property behind the University of the West Indies, which was a part of August Town.

A quiet child, her pet name was "Goodie", while growing up with her two sisters, Gwen and Verona, she told me that she often made her own toys.

She was very creative with her hands, and have left behind carvings, furniture and needlework to prove it.

Although not a great dog lover she liked smooth-haired Fox Terriers and owned one named Peggy.

She loved dancing and music, and her favourite song was

Stardust. She also had a passion for photography and fishing and had her own dark room where she processed her films.

A humble person, she never let on how well she had done scholastically. It was after her death that we found her Senior Cambridge Certificate with distinctions.

Among the things she said to us, her children, were; "the most important thing in life is not a university degree, but to know how to live with the rest of the world."

Her favourite quote from the Bible was "I shall lift up mine eyes to the hills from whence cometh my strength", and her philosophy as a successful landlady, was "It's not the money that matters but the quality of your tenant." These are quotes that my mother has left indelibly in my mind.

She was educated at Conversorium and Tutorial High School. Her working experience included Jamaica Times Newspaper, The Daily Gleaner Spotlight Magazine as well as being a freelance journalist and photographer. Many of her works were published in PepperPot Magazine and The Daily Gleaner.

On January 25th, 1947 Olga Facey married Claude Leslie Pasmore, a Civil Engineer and the union produced four children; Anthony, Paul, Christine and Diane.

It was during this period of her life, when she was being a dutiful mother and wife that she did a lot of her writing and photographing as well as selling real estate.

After an operation in 1975 for breast cancer, her entire life changed. Yet she still had energy to devote her life more to her church by becoming a Eucharistic Minister to "Shut-Ins" and the sick. She never complained about her own physical pain and said it was wonderful to have had an eleven year reprieve when her cancer returned in 1986.

God in His mercy and to give her his twelfth promise took her quickly on the night of the 29th June 1989, when she suffered a massive stroke, and after being blessed by her priest, she went back to Him—the clock chimed, it was 7:50 p.m.

May "The Road of Life" give you as much reading pleasure as it has given me compiling it.

—Anthony Pasmore

SONGS OF CHILDHOOD

The smell of jasmine and wild sage,
The smell of sweet damp earth
And soft wet ferns,
Wild flowers covering the hill
Glistening with dew,
Birds singing in the quiet dawn,
The wind humming through the trees,
The river bubbling and rushing over rocks
The purple mountains rising to the sky...
These were my songs of childhood
Where dreams were weaved...
Those treasured dreams of childhood,
To set them into song
Or on some canvas paint,
That others too could hear,
The music of the woods,
Or keep forever scenes of beauty and eternal joy!
Oh I have not forgotten
The dancing butterflies or shining fireflies,
Which flit across my vision.
They bring tranquility and peace
In these late years
When dreams are filled with fragrance
And the beauty of the hills.

MY TOWN

There are many things to love
In my town,
So many things to see
In my town.
So many wonderful things
To think about,
Laugh about, cry about
In my town.
Peasants on a market day
Singing or dozing in the early dawn
Youngsters, smartly dressed
On their way to school
Filling hearts with hope
For future years;
Adolescent boys and girls
Looking confused and aimless
Speaking guidance to channel
Them into usefulness;
Old and aged people
Still full of dignity and pride
Some broken by years of toil
Or waste or ignorance...
There are ugly things
In my town
Violence and strife

Fear and hate
In my town
But love is strong
And will drive
Fear and hate
Out of My Town, Steamy Side

Rocks on the roofs
To keep the shanties
From blowing away
When the wind is high.

Shanties, low and clustered
Like mushrooms in a row—
Ragged clothes on the line
Breeze blowing through the holes
Taking passage to the hills
And bearded men, animals and children
Searching avidly among the refuse...
Viewing with the crows for a meal,
The truck arrives
The denizens of the dump
Await...
The difference of an empty belly
Or a shirt, a smoke; another wooden crate
To build another shanty by the dump.
The girl in the car speeding by
Puts a delicate handkerchief to her nose...
While the sea murmurs quietly by the shore.

THE BLIND BOY

O cruel fate which makes some
Unsuspecting child lose
The precious glimpse of life
Instead, his only link is
But a touch
Ever so gentle
Cane never reveal
The fleecy loveliness of a cloud
Or yet rich sunlight on a windblown palm
Nor vibrant flame of Poinciana blooms
But sight-less eyes, do not despair
For you are blessed in other ways
You see no fleeting envy in men's eyes
Or wrath, or hunger, tears of anguish
Falling in the night, or wanton lust
Dragging prodigal beauty to the dust
O cruel Fate
Thou has compassion as thy mate.

OLD LADY PICKING BUTTERCUPS

Many mornings as I drive swiftly by
I see an old lady picking buttercups
She looks as fragile as the bloom
Not dressed is she in lavender or lace
Nor yet in rags
But neatly in a worn brown dress

Her hair is silver and her face is quaint
With a beauty and calm from within.
And in my mind I see her room
No palace of tapestry or gold
But golden with sunbeams
Shining on the serenity therein...

Old lady with the silvery hair
I do not know what are your cares
What triumphs, trials or temptations
Have touched you through the years

Passing swiftly I see you merely picking buttercups

AND FORSAKING ALL OTHERS

She hadn't heard from Joe for a very long time. Yes, It was some months now, she hadn't heard at all. The fat old lady of seventy sitting by her radio, in her bed-sitting room, sat thinking. "Fifty years have been a long time" she reflected. "If we had been married, we would have celebrated our golden jubilee last month."

Just then the radio announcer interrupted the programme to say, "We regret to announce the death of one of our well-known sons, Mr. Joe Knight, land-owner and planter of Mandalay Estate, who died this afternoon at the age of eighty, leaving his wife Carmen and two daughters."

The old lady trembled. She heard it, and knew there was no mistake. It was a shock, but at seventy, one comes to terms with the idea of death. She knew he must have been sick or she would have heard or even seen him. She didn't cry, there was only a numb ache deep down inside.

Her friend's daughter, Marcia, came through the door. "Hi, Miss Deborah," she said, but became quiet. She sat down on the chair beside the old woman. The old lady's throat throbbed and Marcia knew she was gathering all the forces within, to control her grief. "Marcia, you hear?" She asked.

"Hear, Miss D, that's why I come over."

"That is good of you, chile, but let it be a lesson to you, me dear." She repeated: "What have I got now? chile, what have I got now? I'm an old woman now, no children, how could I? No one, no one?"

Marcia sat still, for Miss D was talking like no one was there.

"Fifty years is a long time, I was twenty when I met Joe." She looked across the table at the photograph of herself at that time, and then at Joe's. He, in his coat and double-breasted suit, a tall, well-built man in his early thirties. "That was taken while he was in England. He mailed it to me, before he came," she pointed to the picture. "Look at me at twenty, filled with the joy of living, the hope, and the ambition of youth." The face was that of a girl blossoming into womanhood, with slender waist-line, well covered hips. A tail statuesque girl in mid-Victorian dress.

I was twenty then, not pretty but attractive, with a rosy complexion, buxom, proud but poor. Dear Ma had died when 1 was thirteen, and I grew up with an older sister, who had children nearly my own age. I had to forage for myself from that time on, for all she could provide was the roof over my head. I went from one thing to another until I was working in a little fry fish shop in East Queen Street. Then one night it was getting very late and I just decided to lock up, when Mass Joe walked in with three other big men.

They had been drinking, but I could see he wasn't as far gone as the others. You could see they were all rich fellahs, educated, real high class. They ate a lot of the fried fish with plenty onions, and vinegar and pepper, specially Mass Joe: the others were too far gone to eat as much. The others were looking sleepy so Mass Joe said, "Girlie, what time you lock up?"

"1 soon lock up, because I woulda close already only oonoo came in."

"Well, don't lock till I return, I'm going to drop these boys at the hotel and come back and take you home."

"I don't think so, I can fine me way home alone, same as me go every night."

"No you're not going to tonight, though." 1 looked on him and knew 1 would do as he said and must have smiled. Sure enough he came back in a short while and took me home. I saw a lot of him when he was in town. He used to write when he was away in the country, but 1 didn't like to write him, being not educated like him, I was in love with him.

He made me give up the job in the shop and sent me to learn sewing. Then one night we went for a drive out by the sea. It was beautiful moonlight and all a sudden a dark cloud covered the moon. I was afraid, because I knew Joe and I came from very different worlds. He came from a wealthy family, the aristocrats of the island, and what was I? A poor mulatto orphan out of the gutter, as it were. He had taken me out of it, and I was now in a front room, sewing for the neighbourhood, but where would it all end? I knew he could not marry me, or could he?

Then Joe told me what was on his mind. "Deb," he said, "my father is sending me to England. I believe he knows about us, but I don't care; I'm going to help you just the same but don't get wrapped up with anyone until I return."

.About a year later Joe returned. I saw it in the papers: "Mr. and Mrs. Joe Knight arrived on the S.S...." but the tears blurred out the rest.

While he had been away, I had done well with my sewing and with the money he had sent from time-to-time, I opened a little store and was doing good business. I had even paid down on a house, which I later moved into, to avoid Joe finding me.

One day I heard a car at the gate and then who should it be but Mass Joe stepping out and walking straight back into my life, I knew I was being weak, but I still loved him. He was my world. I had never made many friends, because he could only drop in unexpectedly most of the time, I lived only for these visits. He even brought the children to see me once, when they were small. I loved them because they were his, and I thought of them as mine. I knew everything those two girls ever did, and followed their lives from babyhood until their marriages. Yes, I have only lived through the lives of those three people. For the last twenty years, I have not seen so much of Mass Joe. He came one night about ten years ago, with his best friend and told me to get dressed. We went out, all three of us, and he told George, his friend: "See this woman—she has been mine for the past forty years."

I felt good at the time, with him for company, the wine and the dinner, and laughed and was happy that he cared enough to remember. But that night I did not sleep, I kept thinking of my life, how narrow and one-sided it had all been. He did not know the bitterness inside, for the lonely years I had spent, the emptiness, the yearning for the children I never had, the sly look of the other women who knew that I was Mass Joe's woman. How could he know how many times I had wanted to put him out of my life, but could never find anyone quite like him. I had been too much a part of his life."

Marcia saw the old woman's lips trembling and knew it was bound to come. "She hasn't got him now, either," she whispered, then a great unchecked sob came up and shook the woman's heavy shoulders.

THE MORNING STAR AT THE CURSILLO

Green-blue Hills
Clean and cool
Behind the Chapel window;
The Morning Star
Hanging luminous from the sky
"Reach Out and Touch"
It seemed to say
To the beauty of the morn;
The quiet meditation...
The women praying
Silently praising
        God
Feeling His Gentle Presence
In the hush and glory
        of the Dawn.

OUR NATION

Let us rejoice that our Land
Which gave us birth, is blessed
By God's good grace today
To see our nation in its zenith rise
And take its place with dignity
Amid the other nations of the world
Our leaders true, with love and faith
Have fought for freedom's sake
Some have gained, and some have lost,
But all with dedicated lives
Have given to our people
This pride of our dear Land
Which time will fashion with its countless hours
Into a have, where duty, truth and liberty
will be our children's heritage until eternity.

THE CLOCK TOWER

The Clock Tower rises to the sky,
working while the crowd goes by,
each face a varied story
tells of toil, enjoyed or endured.

The half-hour strikes at morning time,
once more the hum of life repeating,
timing each second to fate inexorably
as shutters rise with fresh awakening.

With hands together it dispels
the luncheon hour eagerly,
ever watchful of the minutes
which slip by imperceptibly.

Quickened footsteps happily depart
when at that face they glance,
but leaves it ever vigilant
another day to start.

GOLDEN DAYS

And now the golden Pouie
Sheds its new born blooms
Kissed by the wind
Unseen
To Mother Earth...
And golden dreams
Transcend
The very tree
From which it sprung;
And you,
The purple sprays of Petrea
Cling to its verdant couch
Like some proud matron
With her silvered hair
Bedecked with lilac beads
To suit her autumn years...
For time no longer
Thrusts its erstwhile hand
And regiments her haloed smile
For Spring was yesterday
And Life's full tenure
renews
With soft and trembling lips
Its sacred ties
Of happy days gone by.

MIST ON THE PURPLE MOUNTAINS

Veronica stood on the steps of the old school house and gazed across at the hills, the glorious expanse and immensity of its ridges. Almost purple with a misty veil of white slowly moving across. The stillness, the profundity, absorbed her. She tried to inhale its smell even across the wide expanse of the valley. A feeling of relief at the silence, calmed her first day nerves.

Suddenly her solitude was broken by a faint sobbing coming from the corner of the school-house. She saw a small boy sniffing and sobbing, wiping his face on his shirt sleeves.

"What's wrong Zaccie? How comes you are still here?"

"Is teacher son Larry tek weh me marble dem, Miss. Him bad, just like him big brother."

OLGA MAE PASMORE

"You should have been home already. You had better hurry before it gets dark." She hesitated for a moment. "In fact you had better wait and I will walk with you. Aren't you the one who lives below Burnt Shop?"

"Yes Miss."

They walked in silence for a while, going down the dirt track to the main road. "Miss, I sure you don't know the short-cut to the Big Woods Common? I can show you, if you want Miss."

"I would certainly like to know it," Miss Veronica said. They kept going down through a leafy avenue of pines, fern trees and wild flowers with night shade white-like stars, running on top of the wild plants. Veronica inhaled the clean fresh air, the fragrance of the damp earth, ferns and wild sage and blossoms. She was glad Zaccie had shown her the short-cut through the woods. They came to a small stream, where bulrushes and wild cane waved their tassels with the motion of the wind and the current in the river bed. Up the side of the bank again to a large tamarind tree, whose limbs hung pregnant with long brown pods to the ground. Zaccie picked some quickly. The meat was still bright green. "You want one Miss?" he asked. "No thanks, Zaccie." As they passed the tamarind tree, through the tall thin stalks of fine grass, Zaccie said, "What! Watch Teacher Rasta son a come. Mek we walk fast miss, for him mad, man."

Veronica glanced around and saw the youth. She wondered how he had come upon them without a sound. Zaccie took one glance, and was now running in front of them. The youth swung into stride beside her. She was not afraid. She took a good look at him. Long angular features. Bronze Christ-like face, large eyes, long lashes, soft tuft of beard on his chin. His knitted cap of yellow, green, gold and black, puffed up with the hair under it, his blue banlon shirt and dark pants were immaculate and his feet bare.

"Peace, sister! You the new teacher?"

"Hi, yes."

"Wonder how long you will last with my father's pomposity and dictatorship?" as if talking to himself.

"What did you say Mister?"

"Oh, call me Ras Kuma"

"You from Kingston?"

"Yes."

"Then, tell me something, why you leave the busy metropolis for a poke in the wall like this, "tranquility?"

"Maybe it's the name and the view of the mountains. There is too much rush in the city. One hasn't got time to appreciate the beauty of our land, the peace of mind I believe I will find here. In the city there is the big rush for the bus in the mornings to get to work, the rush to get home, the dirt and filth on the streets, a rot in the hearts of the people a rot everywhere. Oh, it is much better here. It is not crowded."

"The people are not as tranquil as the name of the village though. You better watch out. They are small-minded, greedy, pretentious, hypocritical and pompous. You will see if you stay long enough."

"I do hope I will enjoy working here."

"Hope so. Could I speak to you again sometime, if you won't feel ashamed?"

"I won't."

"See you again."

They had come out to the Parochial Road on which she lived. She turned, but Morgan had disappeared. Where, she did not know. She could see Zaccie in the distance running into his yard beside the shop far down the road.

Earnest Whittle, the young parson for the village, stopped his battered Austin car beside her. "Good evening Miss Davis, hope you are coming to choir practice on Thursday evening?"

"Good evening Mr. Whittle, I guess I will, if it doesn't rain." "And if it does I will call for you. How was school today? Did you like it?" he asked with interest.

"I think so, the children are a little slower than in Kingston but I don't mind."

"Good, I do hope you will stay with us here, as we do need young folks like you in these mountains."

"Thank you," she replied and wondered if it meant for all concerned. Not a bad idea, she thought wildly, but he is a bit par-tic-u-lar, and looks and talks like mummy's only son. Guess I'll find out one of these days.

Thursday night the rain started lightly at first, then developed into heavier showers. That looked like the end of the choir practice for Veronica, however, it stopped and she dressed. Parson Whittle arrived for her. The two fat sisters Mary and Martha, from the other side of the village were with him. She didn't mind Mary but Martha was a bit much for her liking. She worked at the Parochial Office and walked like one of the excavators gathering everything in its path. They were young people she had met at the Guild Club a few nights before. Both were setting their caps for Parson Whittle. She had heard from her landlady most of the gossip in the village.

She wished the girls luck. His ambitions, it seemed, were way beyond them.

He was a Mr. Culture-vulture, not in their mundane world. "One never knows, she thought. Men do such strange things. They were so attentive, so effusive, hanging open-mouthed at his every word, enthralled. The poor guy must feel very flattered."

"Hi, Miss Davis" they called in unison.

"Hello Martha and Mary", she could never remember who was who, they depressed her.

"Mr. Whittle was so kind as to call for us as he was coming from Top Mountain."

Martha gave out as she sat in the car, "You see Teacher son come back to the village. The boy nuh go to town and turn Rasta. Come now to call himself Ras Kuma, but him is stone blind mad. Don't you think so Miss Davis?"

"I don't so, Martha."

"I feel very sorry for him," Veronica said.

"Chut, is a Rasta. Him is too worthless, after all the money Teacher spend on him from him little. Him have no ambition. Him walking up and down the village barefooted, to mek Teacher feel shame, for Teacher is a very proper man."

"Yes, I know that is how you would feel because a hear him was talking to you the other evening."

"Of course. He is still a human being and still Teacher's son, I think. What about the Hippies who are all over our island, do you think they look any cleaner than our Rastas, because they are white?" Parson Whittle gave a soft chuckle. By this, they had reached the Church Hall and Martha did not reply.

During the choir practice, Veronica's mind kept straying, seeing Gaston's aquiline face before her. She looked across the bench and saw the fat self-satisfied mountain of flesh, Martha, who was trying hard to capture Parson Whittle's attention, by grinning inanely all the time. If she hadn't been amused, she could have hated her.

Gaston always seemed to know when she walked through the shortcut in the afternoon, as it was so refreshing after a hard day at school. He would appear soundlessly as if out of a tree, but she was never afraid. They spoke of many things. He told her of his philosophy as some of the "brethren." In principle, it sounded good and very Christian-like. Each man was his brother's keeper and shared what he had with those who did not have, only when he started telling her that Hail Selassie was God, then she ruled his argument out entirely. She could not understand how an intelligent and sensible fellow could have believed that part of the story. The other sore point was the weed. As she put to him, she did not need the weed to digest her religion, as in theory they were both Christians, but maybe the weed was their panacea for their problems.

As sound as her argument was, she could not convince him as he could quote just as much Scripture as herself. Otherwise his argument was so rational. Unless he spoke of his father. She had asked him if he had ever shown his hand carvings to his father. He got into a rage. "He wouldn't understand or appreciate them. He would say I'm a dreamer making graven images. You see, he wanted me to be a Doctor, so he could be proud. He was too dogmatic and prosaic to consider an artist and a doctor in the same breath. You don't understand my father yet." She let it ride, and spoke of other things. Each time they met and talked, she felt so elated, but when he disappeared, she felt what a waste of talent, for he could be guided to become a great artist. If only his father could realize and take him to a psychiatrist. When she thought of it, and how she longed to help, she cursed herself,—"so you think you are a little Jesus, you can cure everybody's ills and fantasies." She was working on his younger brother Larry, who had a wonderful brain but very sadistic tendencies. You better work on him, she thought, he is only eight, Gaston is your own age group, 21-22, you can't help him now. His parents must do that for him.

At Choir some months later, Martha gave out, "You hear what happen to Ras Kuma, Miss Davis?" "No Martha."

"Oh, 1 saw the Police hold him by his waist this evening and bring him into the station, just as I was leaving work and when I asked the men in the yard, they said they found him with Ganja and caught him smoking it in a cave by the short-cut.

"Oh, I'm sorry to hear."

"I know you would, for a hear you and him are friends and him visit you all the time."

"True enough, he is not a bore, he talks intelligently." Deep down she was sorrier for Gaston. She worried whether his father would stand by him now, in his hour of need.

It wasn't long before she realised what Gaston meant by his father's hypocrisy. The next day when he passed her class room, he yelled at her, if she wasn't competent enough to control the children in her class, as they were a bit noisy as usual. Then she asked him if she could start a manual project for the slower members of the group. He barked at her that they would do that when they left school, for there was plenty canes to cut and ditches to dig. She saw him caning the bigger boys in his grade throughout the day.

When he called her into his office, she wondered. He wanted to know if she had known Gaston in Kingston before she came there and if that was why she had taken the job in "Tranquility." He had even heard that Gaston had been to see her the night before. She held her peace. She realized he wanted to find out if she knew Gaston was in jail He made her understand that she had to co-operate with him, whether he was right or wrong. She smiled enigmatically. He was not pleased with her replies for they were non-committal and pert. After school that afternoon, she got a drive into the nearby town to see Gaston, but was not allowed to see him. He had to stay in jail for three weeks as his father never went to bail him.

The morning the case was to come up for hearing, she went to Teacher Morgan to ask him if she could go into town to the dentist. He suspected. He wanted to know who would take her class if she went. She replied then if she dropped dead or got sick, if his school wouldn't go on without her. He cursed her properly, that she was rude and impertinent, and promised to lodge a complaint to the Board, that she had no respect for her elders. She didn't like that at all. She needed and wanted her job. She liked Gaston though, he sent a strange thrill through her whenever they met, but she knew they were not destined for each other. She had had too hard a struggle to come up in the world and had made it practically on her own and would let no one destroy it for her. "If only he could find what he was searching for and get a proper perspective," she thought. She didn't have the time to reclaim him.

She saw so many of her contemporaries putting on this facade to hide their fears, tensions and frustrations, after being pampered and spoilt by parents. She felt that it would pass, like every other phase and in the final analysis, the strong would survive, "I have my little sister to see through high school still, and a grandmother to help, so charity begins at home," she reasoned with herself. When the school board met weeks afterwards and she appeared before it to answer charges of gross incompetence and impertinence, she felt like the ground has slipped beneath her feet... it was then she realized and appreciated the strength and just a little something more about Parson Whittle. He was not the docile mamma's boy she had envisioned all these months. Here was the stronger facet of his personality. He stood up against Morgan and defended her.

He had spoken of things she hardly realized he knew about her. Her great love for the malnourished and semi-retarded children she had tried to bring some sort of pride and sense of achievement into their lives. Her behind-the-scene activities, like visiting parents to enlighten them that children were not chattels and carriers only of wood and water, but that they were individuals who had a new life to live, where values were placed not only on material success, but on the worth of fulfilment of one's self, for they deserved a better life and more exposure to education. That a full week of school served a purpose, instead of the long trek from Thursday to reach the Market and fetch and carry for their parents, while losing precious days of school. This was a speech of which anyone would be proud... She never knew he saw through her excuses of not getting involved with him. She knew it was a small village and the grape vine was faster than telegraph wires.

Teacher Morgan wasn't pleased after Whittle had spoken, and saw the faces of the Education Officer, the M.P. for the

Parish and the Justice of the Peace. They had been impressed and a little over-awed. They all knew Whittle was an honest, conscientious and mature man. At the end, in unison they said, "But Mr. Morgan, Miss Davis is a valuable member of your staff, and if you are not satisfied and willing to work with her, then we could recommend her for promotion to the Junior Secondary School opening in September at Top Mountain. We really find your complaint unjustifiable and considering her on the merits of her work since being here, we feel that your charges could have been laid in a time of anger." "Oh, these young people are too provoking they have no sense of loyalty," was Morgan's gruff reply. He looked with scorn on Whittle and Veronica as if he wished them both dead. "It is left to Miss Davis to decide about the Junior School," the Education Officer ended.

On her way home later, Veronica heard the old Austin behind her, finally stopping beside her. She turned to him, "Well Mr. Whittle, thanks for being such a good advocate. That was very gallant of you."

"It was my pleasure, young lady."

She blushed... "Hop in and let us go to Top Mountain and celebrate with a cool drink. You must be quite hot and exhausted after your ordeal,"

"I think you are right, thanks," and she entered the car. "You know I'm a little sorry for old Morgan, although he pretends that his boy Gaston does not upset him, and has written him off completely, since he drove the boy out of the house two years ago, but I think he was overwrought when they locked up the boy," said Whittle.

"Yes, but he didn't do anything constructive, to help," she replied.

"That's what you think. He was working behind the scenes but did not want the boy to know."

"Is that a fact?"

"Yes, he went to his friends and got the case thrown out for lack of evidence, as it was the boy's words against the policeman's." "True?" but you think Gaston would ever believe that?" "I think most of the boy's behaviour springs from emotional rejection of his father and that is where most of the trouble comes from, as some of the fathers, hardly have any rapport with their sons, so all the sympathies and security must by force come from the mothers, then the boys get all twisted up inside, and revert to whatever is in fashion at the moment."

"Maybe you are being a little too hard on Old Morgan. You know he is the bread-winner and is involved in all the affairs of the school and community, so Mrs. M has to look after the children," Whittle said.

"Yes, but he just gives her the babies and from then on it's her business to bring them up. It's a good thing the other four are girls and there are only the two boys. The young one Larry in my class is quite a case also. Right now, I'm doing my best to straighten him out."

"You know you are quite a thinker Madame."

"Thanks, I'm terribly interested in the psychology of human behaviour patterns."

"I do hope you will use it on our children, when the time comes, and call me down when I slip up as a father."

She was a little shaken as he took her hand in his, and she replied, "I think I will."

OLGA MAE PASMORE

DEEP IN MY HILLS

My roots are on that Mountain Top
      Where the wind blows cool
      Where the colour on the ridges
          dance
      With their shadows
          in the sun
      Where the river slashed
          the foot-hills
      Rushing to meet the sea
      Where the vast expanse of valley
          squatted untenanted by the lea.
          With only animals for company...
          For Time was but a gangling brat
          And that was many a year...
      Now valley, lea and river bed
          are filled
      Far as the eyes can see
The Campus hums like
          buzzing bees
And buildings stretch unending
      Beside the old gnarled guinep tree,
      No river flows by the valley now,
      Only a yawning cavern gapes
      Over this no-man's land
      Gutted and dry with sand.

Yet the mountain still stands
    Tall and strong
Against the radiant sky
The same fresh fragrance
    greets the day
When heavy dew-drops
    Kiss the grass
    And say
Your roots are buried Deep,
Deep in the crags and crevices
    of these hills
These scented, ping-winged, jasmined paths
Which lead me dauntless...
    Into the Great Beyond.

OUR MOMENTS

So little time in which
To whisper the treasured words of love
So little time to take
The tiny flame of happiness that flickers
Through one's Life
And revel in its joys.
So little time to say
The trivial things
Which give true meaning
To this wondrous thing called life...
And so much time for remembering...
Recapturing....
The atoms of joy
In each moment, made precious
By its fleeting charm.

A GENTLE KISS

You pressed your lips against my cheek
Was it in love or pity
Did you seek
To comfort me?

Whether love or pity meant:
Some faery spirit
Must have sent
A gentle kiss
To comfort me.

SOFT MOMENTS

Small hands to lift,
Soft fingers to your face
Soft lips to press,
In a fond embrace.
Tender looks from gentle eyes
To fill a heart with love

THE LEADER OF THE BAND

She makes her debut with a bow
A curtsy to the crowd,
This elfin creature of five years
So self-assured she stands
Lifting her baton high
With perfect ease, keeps time
And thirty tiny eyes and hands
Are guided by her wand.

Some are staring hard at Mummy
Another watches eagerly
to note, if Daddy sees the cymbals
So proud of it, is he
With all their children entice
Precociously she leads.

DRUMS OF CALABAR

Drums rolling,
Beating, throbbing.
Beating in Africa,
Beating like the sound
of her heart,
Inside the Mission House
In that vast land -
Fear of the sound
of the drums;
Throbbing, bursting, searing
Her insides
Black, white,
White, Black...
Parents bringing God
To her black brothers
And the people of Africa
O! Where is the God
They taught her?
Whose image of God
They taught her?
Black, white,
White, black
Like the beating
of her heart
And the drums.

OLGA MAE PASMORE

FLAMBOYANT

Pancho stood under the mango tree, surveying it for a sturdy limb which could take his weight, for the trunk was too wide and straight for him to find a foot hold. At length by climbing the small guinep tree beside it, he hoisted himself and reached a large branch, from which the cherry-ripe fruit came away easily. He plucked the largest of these, filling his pockets, and pushed the rest inside his shirt.

It was cool and comfortable on the spacious branch, his hunger abated, he stretched his six feet odd of body and legs against another limb, pillowed his head on his hands, and closed his eyes. He was trying to think it out for himself, but the breeze and the belly-full of mangoes were too much for his West Indian blood. He would think about it later. Life like this was grand, Mr. Millionaire could never relax like this. His eyes were closing down, and he could not resist.

His sister Ruth was cursing him again, "You lazy good-for-nothing boy, worthless, just want to walk up and down and do nothing for the rest of your life, and people have to work and mine you. You are a man, you not boy anymore. Naomi and miself can't even save two farthing sake of you, for it look like you don't mean to work." He woke and started reflecting. Life was hell, not even your own sisters could understand you. He could not tell Ruth what he really wanted to do, for she would ridicule him. She was cynical. Father's death had embittered and deflated her, because they could no longer live in the teacher's cottage. That was all gone. Only Father would have understood and given encouragement. He liked my drawings and gave me his books of the old masters, Ruth and Naomi were too busy trying to make a living. They were too prosaic. Money, money, everyone was the same, only money had beauty for them. You were lazy, crazy, or a downright bum if you couldn't make it. "Jesus", he thought, I tried. I tried selling men's wear, but could only see the beauty in the faces of the ladies who came to buy it for their men-folk. Bored stiff with the job and the manager, and the whole blasted lot of them.

Nora his old school chum was different. She understood. She helped him with a few dollars whenever she carne into town, to defray expenses and he would take her out. That gave him the train fare to get away from Ruth's nagging. He stayed at her place and roamed the country side and sketched and brought them back to her for appreciation. Yes, they could discuss art and culture and make love on the week-ends by the beach or on some moonlit walk into the woods. She was good but she was a school teacher and wanted respectability. He could not afford either. The panoramic view from the top of the tree was great. The scalloped edges of the hills against the horizon and the mist slowly moving across. A thrill shot through his body.

"This is my country. I must escape beyond myself, and find my soul without fear of life or death. Free myself to do what I want and make something of my life." It was sunset, and the golden sun was sinking slowly in the west. "Yes, I must paint seriously, I must".

While Nora taught school, he combed the country side. It was June, and the poincianas were in bloom. Poet had sung their praises, but he would capture it on canvas. There was a large one over by the big pasture. The land was good to look at. It sloped gently. The rain had washed each blade of grass and leaf and the woods smelt as fragrant and wonderful as a woman powdered and perfumed awaiting her lover. He would never be tired of smelling jasmine and wild flowers, or watching the birds hovering over the lilies in the pond.

His "Poinciana Tree", had brought sudden power and confidence to him. His work became dynamic, rich with colour, vibrant. Each year brought richer rewards, crowned by his one-man exhibition. Fame was his now. The patrons of art had accepted his work. He felt good. Women flocked to his studio for portraits, or landscapes, using that as an excuse to flirt with him. He was conscious of their admiration. It was not conceit but amusement that twinkled in his eyes, enjoying every moment. They gave him no respite, but he did not mind. He had a tender feeling for all women, one had cussed his guts, but one had given him a chance to find his manhood, himself and his self-respect. His sister Ruth was now his secretary. He had sent her children to school after her husband died.

Then Karen walked into his studio one day. Her skin like eighteen century mahogany. Her lips like petals of a bud, opening and inviting. Eyes tender but with a fire and fury of passion, with lashes, long and black. This was beauty, oh but so young, he thought. She looked up to him. He did not smile. "Father told me to come and see your paintings, as I was away when your exhibition took place. May I look at them?"

"You're welcome, I'll show you myself."

He was glad Ruth was out for a change. "I took art at College, but I could never hope to be as good as you are."

"Why should you say that, I'm self-taught, only mixing with the savants when I went to Paris five years ago."

That was how it all started, until her father got wind of it, and forbade her to see him. Pancho could not stand the uncertainty of their trysts for they met whenever possible. He wanted her like he never wanted any other woman before. He just could not have an illicit affair with her. He wanted her for his wife. Her father thought she was too good for him. "Maybe he was right, a rogue like me. A good-for-nothing rogue like me," he thought. He would make her happy, but a year was a long time to wait. She would have to make up her mind or "I will sell everything and go away"!

"Karen, if you don't marry me, it's because you don't love me. You are nineteen now, I have waited one whole year to see if your father would change his mind but he won't, so I guess I'll go so far away, you won't be able to find me." He saw the tears spring suddenly in her eyes, but would not comfort her. After all she wasn't a baby. She must make up her mind.

"No, you can't go away, because you know I love you. It is only father why I hesitate."

"Once we are married, he can't separate us. We can get a special license, so it won't be published."

"Yes, but what will I do for clothes, I won't be able to get them out of the house. I won't even have a gown."

"Oh, so you will be my bride after all, gown or no gown. I'll have Ruth and Naomi look after that and your trousseau. You can talk it over with them and you three women can select your things." His sisters had done everything for the wedding and were intrigued at the elopement. It was spice only their brother could provide.

Pancho leaned back against the pillow and tried to get up but felt the pain again in his stomach.

"Curse this damn ulcer."

"What is it dear?"

"Nothing much my love, only that confounded jab in the stomach, reminding me I'm not as young as 1 was."

"Oh Panch, you must see the Doctor again, as the diet doesn't seem to be of much help."

"Karen, my sweet, I guess you are sorry you didn't marry one of the boys your own age."

"Don't ever say that again."

"I know, I'm an old bag now, two years of this heavenly bliss and I have caved in on you, I shouldn't have persuaded you to marry me."

"But I didn't need any persuading, I only wanted to be sure. When you were willing to chuck everything over for me, then I knew it was for real, like me."

She leaned across the bed and kissed him. His face was hot and moist with perspiration. She took out a clean pyjama shirt for him and he put it on. "I'll go down to the studio next week, I'll just take a little rest this week." "Yes and tomorrow I'll go with you to the Doctor and get this ulcer off my mind. By then I'll be fit, don't get worried Karen, I'll be all right."

"I'm not worrying, but I wouldn't like anything to happen to you, I'd die too."

"Oh no, you wouldn't, you would find some handsome young man and marry as soon as I was cold."

"Panch, if you say that again, I'll punch you right where it hurts, you devil."

"Never mind Karen, you will learn, honey, life is much bigger than both of us. Let's go for a drive in the hills, and have lunch, I'm not that sick, you can drive."

"That would be lovely, but you should be resting at home."

"I'll be resting all the same. We'll take the blanket and I'll read or sleep while you sketch, the fresh air will do us both good."

"It's a deal, I'll be ready in a few minutes."

The drive up into the hills was pleasant. She drove at a comfortable speed taking the tortuous, winding road with unhurried ease. They stopped to look at the view of the harbour across from the valley, and the mountains of differing greens almost coming towards them.

"I never get tired of the hills, fact is I feel better now. This is just what I needed to perk me up. I think it's those damn portraits which are getting me down, spending most of my time on them, but that's where the money comes. Someday I'm going to build a cabin out here, away from civilization, very primitive, eh Karen? I guess you would get tired of it in a month. No theatre, no cocktail parties or any of those props to living, just clean fresh air."

They found a little knoll covered with grass, and within easy reach of the car. Karen settled him against the trunk of a tree with blanket and cushions.

"You fuss over me as if I was 21 and you were 40..."

"I want you to be comfortable my darling, then I'll leave you to rest, while I go and sketch."

Pancho didn't mind her going, he wanted time to think... He knew he would never tell her what the doctor had said. "Two more years for you young man. I'm sorry to say your ulcer is incurable." He didn't have to spell it out. He cursed himself, "that's the price you pay, louse, for a nice young wife who really loves you. Bad living, louse... Better luck next time louse, but there isn't too much time left louse only two years, twenty-four months louse." He brushed a tear away, as Karen came into view. "Hey, let me see what you did?" "Was it my sleeping mountain, or my purple hills that kiss the sky?"

"Oh you romantic goat, it's a white patoo I saw in the Flame Tree."

"Karen, I was just thinking, let's take the most luxurious boat and cruise around the world? Will you enjoy that with an old romantic goat for company?"

"Oh Panch, she ran and hugged him tightly, I'd love nothing better."

FOR MY FRIEND ELSIE

There is no grave
On which to place,
A rose for you.
But in our hearts
You have left a
Garden filled with Buds
Of course, strength and hope
To those you loved.
And a silent prayer
          goes up
That someday, we will see
 The golden sun-rise dawn
   In God's beautiful Eternity.

A TRIBUTE TO MCARTHUR IRELAND

Gone forever is that fertile mind
Which had the patience and the pride
Of imparting to lesser beings,
The love of knowledge,
The romance of the lands
      of France and Spain
A veritable Genius, one could not disdain.
He brought alive the History of the past
with vivid pictures which were sure to last
You saw him march with Caesar's army
      cross the Alps,
Heard him recite the beauty
      of Cicero's thoughts, at home
And wished you too had lived in
      ancient Rome
And do agree with B. St. J
Oh! would by some magic,
      that expansive brain
Could with Posterity remain.

LA CHAUMIERE

A small cafe in rustic setting
On the side of the road in Molieu
Young gay laughter drifting...
The warmth of Madame
Pervading the place,
Large, wooden platters
Filled with mussels, crabs
And shrimps, served with
Slices of lemon,
White wine from Bordeaux
And Monique's eyes dancing
With mischief...
Oh, we were happy and care-free
And one with music
Of French songs of love,
The girl with long brown hair
Playing the piano...
The people at the bar
Humming the tunes
Eyes sparkling...
Lips met with summer kisses
The "joi de vivre"
Enchantment of France
And her lovers.

ROSIE

Rosie lifted the hand of bananas gently, carefully putting them down on the wooden stand at the gate of the little cottage. She paused each time she came out, looking down the road, until she was reminded by the rasping voice from inside the cottage, "Gal a whey you da look fa down de road, come back fe de res a banana noh? You ever hear—whey sweet nanny-goat run him belly?"

Rosie kissed her teeth in an undertone, and turned reluctantly towards the door again. She pouted her pretty mouth, then dropped the last hand of bananas hastily on the table grumbling to herself, "You can sey what you like, if you link a gwine stay ya all de days a mi life and get crumogin like you, you fool."

A large American car came swiftly around the bend of the country road, its occupants sunburnt and prosperous looking.

Rosie lifted one hand of the bananas and rushed along the side of the road, "Ripe bananas lady and genklemans."

One of the men in the car said, "By Gad she's cute. Let's get a picture Sam." Already Sam had seen the picture and had his 35 mm camera focused in the direction of the girl.

"Here kid, take this for the picture; we don't need the bananas today," one of the men said, handing Rosie a crisp dollar bill.

Rosie crushed the note lovingly in her palm, looking to see if her step-mother had seen when the tourist gave it to her. She had made up her mind that it was hers for keeps for they hadn't bought the bananas. She went back to sit on the wooden stool by the gate. The woman called from the house, "How much you get, a hear a car stop awhile ago".

"Dem didn't buy no banana, mam."

"Gal meck you lie so."

"Dem didn't buy no banana, dem only sey a pretty."

"You lie, dem teck you pitcha den, an dem gie you money."

"No mam."

"A doan believe a wud you say, you too lie an bad, you sidun dey tink sey you pretty an so lazy, you tink pretty can pay? If you think sey is so life go, you fool."

"Come look no mam, you no see sey de banana dem sidun same way as you gie me dem."

"A ooh? So is pose you a pose fe pitcha, you tink you pretty? What a poppy-show, what a joke," and she laughed with derision.

"Ole fool, all de bwoy dem sey a pretty," Rosie reassured herself quietly.

The woman turned back into the yard, while Rosie sat fingering the white coffee rose in her blue black hair. After a little while a boy came up the road running an old iron hoop steered with a piece of wire. Rosie called out to him:

"Rupert come sid down ya fe me, a soon come back".

'Awright, mine you meck Aunt Liz lick off me head when she doan see you dough."

"She's awright, she gawn down a de fence line, when she do come up back tell her a gone change de place whey de goat tie out."

"Mine de goat buck you."

"You too fass."

"A bet a leave de banana dem an meck her see sey you gone fe meet Syl."

"Shee," she put her finger to her lips," "Satiday night you we wan bulla."

"Lawd yes, a coulda eat one right now," but Rosie was already walking down the road. A group of men were sitting on the parapet wall by the road. One tall, well built youth sat by himself on the other side, under a tree. Rosie passed delighted at the sight of the men watching her as she swung well rounded hips and hummed a tune. One called "Hi, Rosie, stop dey no, I wan see you."

"Cho oonoo leave de pickney alone," an older one said.

"You no know she just bawn yestiday."

Rosie smiled coyly throwing a glance in the direction of the tree where Sylvester sat strumming his guitar. She walked on, and at the bend of the road stopped; listening for the approaching twangs of the guitar. She did not have to wait long for them. She heard the deep crooning voice of Sylvester and the strumming of the guitar, and a thrill ran through her body. She kept walking slowly then. Sylvester caught up with her still strumming the guitar, not saying anything until she turned off the main road into the little track. "You like that song?" he asked.

"Yes, what it name?"

"Rosie."

"Story."

"No. true, is you a meck it for."

They sat on the grass under one of the huge plum tree.

"Well sing it meck a hear no,' Rosie said.

'Awright, but you gwine laugh."

He started crooning softly,

> "O Rosie you be true to me
>
> Even if your Ma should see
>
> Me kissing you beneath de tree
>
> An box you up for it."

He sung it to the tune of "If you will marry me, me, me, if you will marry me."

She laughed and said "Play it again Syl," bubbling with mirth. Sylvester laughed too, saying, "Don't is true?"

He played it again and many of the new songs hits while Rosie settled herself comfortably on the grass, cupping her chin with both hands and looking up at him with worship and love shining in her eyes.

He stopped playing, putting the guitar on the grass beside him. Rosie said, "You ask Miss Ruby bout the job at the hotel fe me?"

"A couldn't get fe see her Satiday night for she was with a heap a tourist people dem at de table an it woulden look nice fe I go up to ask her bout it dat time."

"Well den tell me bout Satiday night noh."

"Yestiday mawning me and Sam go up with the guitar dem, and we ask Mr. Stewart if him need any more waiter dem fe de night, so me so lucky de head-waiter come out to him and sey yes, him can teck on one man fe help dem because de hotel full an dem have a big crowd. So me tell him sey Sam is me pardner and if him can; meck we do a number in de-floor-show, so him sey maybe, kina casual like, you know. Sam and me do de number Answer Me', an after dat a Calypso, an him sey when we finish it 'not bad'. By dat time a couple of the guess dem can gader round, when a singing, and clap when a done, A go back dere in de evening and help de waiter dem at twelve a'clock when de floor show start me an Sam do 'Banana' and dem encore an den I sing 'Changing Partners'. Mr. Stewart give me 15/-fed e singing an ten shillings fe help de waiter an tell me him we use me pon Satiday night time."

"A only hoping you can get de job up dey fe me for me caan stan Aunt Liz much longer, she too miserable. All a bun her is because me won't notice de short big belly Jabez, she faver him coulda be me Poopa, jes because him have nuff goat an cow an piece a lan up by de riverside. Every evening when a sidun out a gate him a come an stan up, want talk to me, den Aunt Liz she a come out when she see me cut me eye after him. Hear her noh Syl, 'Miser Jabez, you noh know when dem is young dem is foolish, she wi soon get some sense in her head', dat is in her bess voice, she put on, a was bus out a laugh dat time. Him faver dem big saw-back green lizard when dem a crawl pon de mango tree."

"You mine she doan meck you married him."

"She woulda haf fe tie me an carry me to de alta".

"Sure? Him have money an me no have noting, not even shoes. Is Joslyn own me borrow fe go up a de hotel lass night."

"Well, you soon can buy one, an I don't have none either", she said regretfully.

He drew her to him and her lips were moist and ready. They were oblivious to the cows looking on with bovine acquiescence. His long sensitive fingers caressed her while their unfettered toes shared the ecstasy. Getting up suddenly she said, "Let we go back now, what a way it get dark quick," as she brushed the burrs from her skirt.

"An hope Aunt Liz don't box you up in truth for a won't have nobady to kiss again."

"Gwan, a who you da fool an, an de coolie-gal up de shop have her eye pon you long time."

"Yes, you know she not bad," he teased.

"Dats awright I have Jabez, member".

He gave her a nasty look.

Aunt Liz was calling the girl "Rosie." Burp, burp... "Yes, ma."

"A what happening to you eeh?"

"Nothing ma."

"Den meck you couldn't answer me?"

"Me was coming, ma."

'A ho, you must a tink me fool. You better come and clean out de room. Mister Jabez coming here dis evening, and a hope you going talk to him properly—No badder fool, for him have nuf cow and goat upa de river side so you can stay de an fool—All

Sylvester can gie you is a baby an noting to mine it. For next ting him go whey and leave you wid it an dem man nowadays naw teck you an pickney fe mine, you hear gal?"

Rosie managed to clean the room under the watchful eyes of her step-mother. She 'johnny-cuppered' extravangtly—the floor shone like glass when she had finished with it. When she got up her old dress was covered with the dye of the bark she had used, and her hands, her beautiful honey-coloured hands were red. She looked on them and winced. Tor Jabez"—poor Aunt Liz wonder if she suspected, she was smart—trying to rush her into marrying him, so she would be comfortable with the cows and goats for company, while she had to endure Jabez for a lifetime, she thought. A big boar grunted and passed her while she stooped by the side of the wooden cask to wash her hands, she looked and said softly, "Yes Missa pig no wonder a hate pork, you fava him fe true."

After lunch Aunt Liz said, "See if you see Rupert and beg him come pick two jelly, as a want to offer Jabez when him come. While you doing dat I wi go down a Miss Lou so buy a bottle a Captain Morgan so a can offer him a drink. You haffe sweeten him up and do like de rich folks up a de big house, when anybody come to dem, dem offer dem whisky and rum an sey dem a entertain—so chile don't you mecking up you mine?" And she became confidential and almost pleasant.

"Him is a very nice man you know, him use to treat the coolie girl him did have one time, good you see. Him gie her iron-bed, an wash stan an heap a clothes an shoes, an poor unfortunate manfi one day she run wey wid a real ole wutless bwoy go a town. A see her after dat, she mash up, she mash up so tell, a never even turn like a know her. She so shame she never show her face back in de village after dat. She must dead by dis, for she did fava like John-crow roas plantain. Well it lef to you gal, you betta meck up you mine, an teck advise."

"Yes ma," Rosie said, "A gwine go call Rupert, a believe him did pass go a school dis marning."

Rosie had to restrain herself from running until she was out of sight of Aunt Liz. She went in the direction of the school and met Rupert running with a group of boys. "Hi Rupert", she called, "come here little."

"You wan see Sylvester. A just see him pass wid a bundle in him han," he said between gasps.

"No man, go down de yard but teck you time till you finish play and pick two jelly, teck dem and put at the back step fe me and if you see Aunt Liz tell her a soon come back. A gone fe pick some lily up a de pond side fe dress up de house."

'Awright Rosie, bring a bulla fe me."

"Yes man", and she walked briskly up the road. She turned in the direction of the little hut upon the hill and whistled. Sylvester came out in a clean shirt and pants sporting a new pair of brown shoes. "Come Rosie, a pack up you tings see the grip a buy it fe eight shillings clear up de Bay, because Miss Lou woulda ask me if a going a town,"

Rosie said, "You know a woulda just like fe peep through de window an watch Aunt Liz face dis evening when Jabez come." "You too bad gal", he replied. "Come a show you something, when you change you dress."

Rosie ever curious quickly drew the dress over her head and came to the door. Sylvester had his fist closed, told her to shut her eyes, then he said, "Open you eye and teck a look." Rosie opened her eyes. She saw a tiny band of gold and was dumb. Two big tear drops hurried down her cheeks.

When she found her voice she said, "Sylvester, a didn't know you was so good, a glad you see, Aunt Liz won't get fe laugh afta me now, she jus' dun tell me sey all you have fe gimme is a pickney an run wey fef me."

"Feget her now my darling meck we get de bus to St. Ann's Bay Father sey we must reach de church by five o'clock."

MR. GILOU

I do not know what strange Fate
Brought you into my Life,
What enigmatic alchemy
of your existence
Sent you into my heart
I only know you as "un petit patriot"
Now being reared, with loving care
By friends, in some secret place
In your Father's land
A Land being torn by civil strife
By man's distorted Fears and deadly hate,
Where honest men are killed
        or from their land exiled.
Where Freedom is a Phantom
        and truth no longer lives.
Yet one day in the far flung future
Who knows, or who will prescribe?
You might be the Leader of a new and better world
Cleansed by the blood, the tears, and torments
of you father's friends
In this your ravished land'
And then with all your heritage
Your culture and hauteur
Will lead your abject people,
With the new light of Freedom
The Torch of love
And joyously proclaim
"L amour est fort comrne la mort"
The seed which grew and nurtured
From the heart of L'Overture.

OLGA MAE PASMORE

THE LEADER OF THE GANG

Peter Larkin swaggered down the lane with confidence and mischief dancing on his face. He had been the first to see the truck turning up the street, and it was loaded.

He let out a loud whistle and gates slammed two seconds afterwards, the gang falling in behind him. He was leading the attack with precision. Every man was armed. "Man-boy, you and Scissors cover the north. Boots, you and Rufus, below the steps. Fonso, you teck the south."

"Right, Peter."

The driver of the truck backed up to the steps of the bakery door. The sidemen lifted and packed the bags of flour and sugar in perfect rows of ten. They called out through the mesh door to the men inside. "Fifty flour and twenty sugar. Call the foreman to come check it".

The old foreman counted the rows quickly and said, "Go round and get the book sign."

The truck drove off. A few minutes later, Foreman Goldson called to the men to come and carry the goods into the storeroom. "We soon come, the dough soon finish rolling off."

In the meantime Larkin and the gang had raided with dexterity and had floured up the lane at bird speed. By the time, the old foreman came out and opened the door, he saw that something was wrong.

Foreman Goldson called out to the boss. "Half bag of the flour gone, sah!"

"Don't be a fool, Goldson. You crazy, man? You just call out and said you checked it and Miss Rose signed the book for it. So what you coming with now?"

"Yes, sah, dem was right, 'cause de man dem pack them in tens but them cut the bag on the outside, and tek more than half, an 'bout three of the sugar bag dem cut too."

"Don't joke, Goldson you go look again. The rum must be dim you eye. Not in so short a time."

"A tell you sah, the bag dem cut. If you tink is lie check it, sah."

"Check what? What the hell you think ah paying you for?"

"But you know sey Larkin and him gang dem bad, sah. And 1 never tink sey dem coulda move the tings like lightning."

"You know something, Goldson? The next time this happen you

going pay for it. Not one rahtid penny of my flipping money going to lose again. I pay you to check the goods and see them in order when them come. Not for hell when the truck come you don't put tail-end at the door and get the men to teck up the goods before Larkin and him gang them strike."

"If I ever catch that Peter Larkin, ah strangle him with me bare hands! As ah live and breathe, you watch me!"

"In fact, Goldson, you better walk up the lane and look if you see any of the gang and try and find out if is them really teck the flour. See if them in the area. It must be them. Ah bet you would know what number drop-pan play but you don't know who teck the flour. Just find out 'bout me flour and sugar!"

"Awright, Missa Jackie, ah gone find out, sah. If them up there, I wi know. My spy them up there to, O.K., sah, I wi find out."

"You better find out and soon, you worthless no-good!"

Goldson went quickly down the steps, too glad to get out of range of the further lambasting he was going to receive, if he remained.

Everything was quiet on both sides of the lane. As he reached the gate where Larkin lived, he peered through the peep-hole at the top, which had string drawn through to secure the latch. Suddenly, he heard something like a stone whizz through the air. It landed right in front of him, where it exploded.

He didn't wait for another sign. He was on his way at a sprint to the end of the lane. Then he circled and trotted warily down the lane until he came back to the main street. There he tried to regain his composure.

At the corner, he asked Oven-man Levi, who was catching a

breath of cool air on the sidewalk, what number the Drop-pan had played.

Levi said, "Nuh number five."

"Me Gawd! nuf tief? Me buy young gal 16 and married woman 32. Me never tink bout the goods whey lose. You know, Jeffrey dose off round de back and tell me him dream bout people bawling fe police and I never tink bout the flour dem brute tief. Bwoy, a coulda win bout six dollar today, instead, ah getting a good cussing from Missa Jackie. You did have the 5, Levi?"

"No, Foreman, mi no catch it neither."

"Levi, you nuh thirsty, man? I coulda drink a whites before Missa Jackie see me again. You have money, man? Come buy me a whites. You did catch de pan yesterday. You tink a didn't hear, nuh?"

"Awright, Foreman, come nuh," Levi replied,

They walked quickly towards the rum shop on the other corner and ordered their "whites,"

A man stood by the counter. He called out: "Hi, Goldson, ah hear you need a machine-man inside dey, is true? How it go?"

"True?" Missa Ran and his old, wrinkled face took on a look of cunning. "We have to get a man, 'cause is me milling de dough mose of de time, since we fire Ken, an me too ole now fe set dough, mix it and turn round run machine. Slim help me out some time, but him have fe him work fe do. Anyway, master, you know how it go awready. A wi talk to the boss. You know somebody?"

"Yes, man, ah have a guy name Papa-Son. Him good back a

demachine so tell. Him work plenty place, but him granmodder dead de odder day and him went to de country. When him come back, him never get back de job."

"Ah guess you going collect to, like miself."

"No, man, is me fren."

"O.K.," and he downed the rest of the 'whites', "Come, Levi, Missa Jackie mussie cussing like de devil by this time."

Levi answered, "Cho, him caan say nothing to me, for me tek three load a bun out a de oven since mawning and de other batch caan ready yet."

"Yes, master, but him setting for me. Like how him flour and sugar gone, him is like any bad bull."

They slipped up the steps and Goldson turned quickly by the side of the building.

The girl Rosie in the office spied Goldson as he slipped by and called out, "Foreman, you find them?"

"Shh, ah soon come. Missa Jackie inside?"

"No, he is gone in town."

Goldson came back in a little while.

"You found the boys dem?"

"No, Miss Rosie. By the time me walk by Larkin gate, dem throw bum after me and me have fe run. Dem boy is bad boy."

"Tell me something, Foreman. Do you ever think that those boys could be hungry? You know if they have parents? Tell me about the leader, Larkin. How old is he? Where are his parents?"

"Him bad. Him poor modder have fe work, for him father dead and is a whole heap of dem, but him is the smallest. Him an him gang dem jus' bad, Is dem tief de flour."

"Foreman, tell me something. You ever give those boys any of the bun and cake that return?"

"Cho, them woulda tief in any case. The bwoy dem wile like any deer, dem only wan' tief,"

"Awright, Foreman, next time when you see Larkin, call to me and let me know him."

Rose heard a noise down the lane and looked through the office a few days afterwards. She saw about six small boys fighting and raising hell in general. She heard one of them cry out, "Lawd, you kick me, Peter."

They were all about eight or ten years old. She could make no mistake. He was the leader, though no bigger than the others. In fact, he was leaner but stronger looking and had an air about him.

A pixie-shaped, slate-coloured face with soft reddish-brown hair on top. Thin wiry legs in torn khaki pants with his little black buttocks protruding.

He had something to eat in a piece of paper and the others were swarming around, begging and fighting him for it. He kicked and swung his arms right and left, and managed to push the last piece of the food down his throat.

Rosie called through the window, "Peter, come and I'll give you some cake."

"No fooling, you want Missa Jackie buss me head, nuh?"

"I wouldn't fool you. Honest, come up and I'll give you some."

"No miss, you going tell Missa Jackie fe try catch me, so him can beat me ."

"I'll keep my word, believe me."

He shook his head. "Never dat!"

"O.K. I'll put it on the steps, since you don't believe me."

"Awright, but when Missa Jackie drive out an gone."

Rosie got busy after that, but when she looked later, the paper bag of bread and cakes had gone.

Every day she put a bag on the steps and it would disappear. She never knew when Peter took it, but she would hear the squabble under the window when the sharing took place.

One day she decided not to put the bag on the steps, but to keep it in the office. He must have crept up the steps and not seeing the bag he called softly, "Miss Rosie!" She held out the bag to him. He snatched it quickly from her hands and ran down the steps,

She heard the voices under her window, but there was no fighting. Peter was busy doling out to the five boys when she looked.

A STRING OF FISH

Mr. Ramsay had arranged to give Gussie work for a few days. He had drunk a little bush tea and left the hut by dawn so as to reach Mr. Ramsay's property by seven, to start work. He only wished he would be able to pick up another Job after this one, so that he could pay his way to Kingston. The work was sporadic and uncertain. Each time he had collected a few shilling he had to use it to buy food and so could not save enough to buy the pair of blue-jeans and the plaid shirt hanging in Miss Mattie's stall in the market on Saturdays. He was sure he would be able to buy the clothes this time because he heard they would be starting work on the road next week. He would go down on Monday, for Mr. Ramsay's fencing would be finished by Friday.

The twenty-eight shillings he earned from running the fence looked good to him that Friday and he went immediately to pay Miss Beckie for the salt Fish and mackerel he had bought for dinner during the week. On Monday he went down the little track leading from his hut out to the main road. His toes went down in the mud and it stuck to his feet. It would peel off as he went along. When he reached to where the road forked, a few men were already there lolling on the bank, or sitting with their machetes between their legs. He saw his friend Baboo leaning by a tree and went over to him. "Hi, what you know bwoy?"

"You see the boss-man yet?"

"Him naw come ya now, we just ha fe wait."

Later, the short stocky man came out from the small wooden building across the road,

"Boss," Gussie attempted to address him.

"Awrite, jus gie me a chance, the headman wi call you when a ready."

"Solomon," he bawled.

"Yes, Sir."

"Get those things out the car."

The boy Solomon came running, answering quickly, "Yes, Sir," and jumped with alacrity.

The headman came out about an hour after that, with a sheet of paper, calling in a strident tone the names of the labourers he needed. Gussie wondered if by the time he got to the W in Warren he would have had all the men needed, as that usually happened.

He was lucky this time, "Agustus Warren".

"Yes, Sir," he answered, breathing a sigh of relief, he would be able to go to Kingston after all.

Icilyn his sister had written giving him the address where she had her room, promising if she could get off she would meet him at the bus terminus. Kingston must be a nice place he thought. Look how Icilyn had returned looking completely different. Her hair was ironed out and she had so many new dresses and a ting call "nylon" stocking and blouse.

Gussie had bought the coveted pair of jeans and plaid shirt. He wrapped the old pair in the clean bit of brown paper which he smoothed with deliberate and loving care. He was leaving the little hut he had wattle himself; it was nothing to leave behind he mused; someone passing could take shelter under its thatched roof. He couldn't bother to take the two burnt pans in which he cooked his meals; it wasn't much use taking the crocus bag that had covered the wooden bed whose legs were buried in the ground. These were his only possessions and they weren't worth taking along.

He stepped through the door of the hut and walked down the track leading to the Main Road, His feet felt imprisoned in the white crepe sole; it was not burning him but being unaccustomed to it, his toes sought the freedom they had previously enjoyed. He was going to Kingston now, not leaving any bills behind. He had paid Mr. Ramsay the ten shillings for the lease of the square of land, and he was the only person he had told he was leaving, as he wasn't renewing the lease. No one would even, miss him, only perhaps Miss Beckie. She would miss the few shillings he had spent with her when he worked. Baboo couldn't care less for Gussie had never accepted his invitations to go to the bar with him on Fridays to drink out the few coppers when he had them. None of the men in the village cared much for him because they said: "Cho man, you no talk so nobady no know wey you tinking, you too quiet man, nobady caan know you dey bout."

"Dem is awright; when you chat too much de 'ole a dem know you business," he thought to himself.

"Dem always boasting how dem go a Kingston all the time and the nice time dem have. Well I gwine, but I gwine save mi money till a get enough to buy couple square a lan' and put up me own room and hall." These were the thoughts which ran through his head as he walked down the road. He was going out to the junction—where the bus stopped to await passengers going to Kingston—all the while feeling his pocket to reassure himself that the twenty shillings were still there. He could hear the bus racing down the road, its brakes screaming as it came to a standstill on the asphalt.

Gussie crossed the road on to the side of the bus. The conductor climbed up the little ladder at the back, to arrange the baskets on the top to make space for those arriving! "Hurry up oonoo come aan an mek we lif up go a town. Caledonia pass fe you give me, is like a like you why a teck fe you fus," he addressed the fattest woman in the crowd.

"Gwan, you can facey wid mi and see whey me man do you," she replied. "Tap ma, you caan mek joke noh, mi no man to?"

"You really mus a "man-to," fi mi man favour Goliat, no every man can pilot dis ya boat yah bwoy, jes put mi basket good, no mek it drap off you hear mi love?"

Gussie stood a little off by himself. The other three women handed up their crocus bags and baskets. Then timidly he went up to the conductor, "How much it cos fe go a Kingston, sah?"

"Seven bob; you wan go—you got de cash?"

Gussie counted the seven shillings gingerly dropping them in the man's grubby palm.

"Awright you can go teck you seat now."

He went quickly and awkwardly and settled himself into the corner of the back seat. On the other seat facing him was Joshua, who lived down the road from him. He called out to Guss, "Hi, man, how you neva tell me you gwine a town, meck you ceitful soh?"

"A gwine go look fe Icilyn, me long fe see her."

That was all Joshua could get out of him. He didn't think talking was necessary so early in the morning. Joshua could find a lot of people who felt like chatting. Some of the women chatted steadily most of the time, while others sat relaxed, resting their chins on their chest, sleeping off quickly as only peasants could, despite the noise and the jerking of the bus. The conductor and Joshua kept up an argument; first it was the Election, the new motor-cars, the sudden exodus of the people going to England. The conductor said, "A woulda like teck a chance miself, but a fraid, cause a hear when cole go fe bite you, you caan do anything bout it."

"If it was Merica we would a go rite now, but me noh able fe sell me couple piece a ting to go, den when mi reach, me no like de place and me so shame me caan come back. Some a dem lucky dem get throo, but puss an daag, noh have de same luck."

"Life hard anyway you tech it, the naga dem tink sey you can pick up money pon de street everywhere else besides Jamaica, it jus waiting fe dem pick it up. It good fe dem go see all de same, for dat is di only way dem wi learn."

Gussie listened but kept silent. He thought Kingston would be quite enough for him. He was already dreading the uncertainty of his decision to go, and the anxiety he felt if Icilyn was not there at the terminus to meet him, worried and perplexed him. The bus stopped at each town, and some of the passengers came out, stretched their legs or went in to have a drink at the bar. Gussie was hungry so at one of the stops he went into a shop; his eyes roved over the glass case where the bread and cakes were kept. He saw just what he wanted, "Give me two flitters and quattie bread." The golden-brown fritter disappeared simultaneously with the bread into the cavern of his mouth, which he wiped with the tiny piece of paper in which the woman had handed him the goods, for she had not wrapped them. He wanted something to "Wash-down" the food, but could not spare the sixpence for a soft drink. Instead he went further down the road, to the stand-pipe and drank thirstily. He felt as if he could not drink enough of the water; his belly was full now but his lips still held the salty tang of the fish from the fritter. Nothing to be done about it. He went back and took his seat in the bus. By 2 o'clock, he thought he would reach Kingston.

The driver at last took his seat and new passengers came, pushing and arranging their baskets whenever they could find space. Gussie thought—women could always be relied on for a state of confusion and jabbering...jabbering; they spent more than half their lives chatting.

The bus was moving now at a terrific speed as if the engine itself had taken a few. The women were calling out to the driver, "Hi, massa mek you a drive so fas? Teck time noh." Instead of heeding them he put on a little more speed. They raced along, the tyres screaming on the asphalt,

"Oonoo mus' a doan waan reach Kingston todae," the driver replied,

When they came to the next town they stopped again. Gussie

looked through the window of the bus at the clock in the Chinese shop before which they stopped; it was after one o'clock. For more than half an hour they remained there, the passengers getting more and more restless; the women eaten up with anxiety.

"Lawd, but whey the driver gone to again," one said.

"Cho, him no mus a gone fe drink more rum," another gave out.

"Demya man now a days all dem can tink of is the rum drinking, dat's why me prefer fe come ina de dray aldough it teck longer," an old woman said.

Caledonia remarked, "Same as the bus have fe refuel, is same way so the driver him have fe refuel."

"Come awn. Driver," a few of the women yelled in the direction of the bar.

At last they saw him come out of the bar wiping his mouth and hands with his red handkerchief and enter the bus. He started off again. This time Gussie was terrified; he held on to his seat until the veins stood out on his hand. One of the women said, "Lawd Jesus, do meck we reach safe." The bus kept on the road miraculously, swaying from one side to the other. As it settled itself in the middle of the road a loud explosion followed. One woman bawled, "Lawd me dead done."

Beckie called out, "Manda, you dead?" as some of the women fell off their seats.

"Me no dead but me 'peechless" was the terrified reply. They were only shaken and the bus had come to a sudden stop. Everybody yelled out, "Whey happen Driver?"

"Cho, oonoo too coward, is only a blowout me get and dat oonoo mus expect," he replied. "Oonoo come out and sid-dung pon the roadside. Mek we go fi fix it."

They grumbled and lamented but took themselves off to the side of the road. Gussie was upset now, knowing he would not reach Kingston until late. He dreaded the very thought. Icilyn would never wait until it got so late at the bus stop.

The conductor and some of the men were fixing the tyre while the driver stretched his full length on the grass under a tree and in a second, it seemed, emitted a succession of snores. It was practically impossible to believe that such nuances of sound existed. His mouth opened, and the snore seemed to reverberate from his larynx into his nasal passage, playing a staccato medley.

The new tyre was now put in place, but it had taken quite a time as the men were in no particular hurry; neither were the lug spanners. Some were too small while others were too large, and it was not until they were able to borrow the right sized spanner from a bus coming in the opposite direction, that the nuts were tightened, the hub caps put back in place. The conductor shouted, "We ready now, oonoo can come siddung back," while he went up to the prostrate driver and tried to awaken him. The driver uttered an incoherent groan and rolled over on his side. The conductor in a peevish voice said, "Mi caan wake him."

Caledonia, who had not yet returned to her seat in the bus, said, "Leave him to me; mi wi wake him, mi can wake di dead, much less him."

It was no idle boast. As she threw her full weight on him, the driver open his eyes, squinted, looked around uncertain of his bearings until he regained a standing posture stretched his hands above his head and twisted his body, with his mouth opening in a super-yawn. "Whey happen, is earthquake? he asked. "Lawd, sleep sweet sah! a feel good now."

Caledonia said. "Is only me touch you me love, for we waan go a town."

"Whey you say? Touch? Look ya, me tink say is shake the earth a shake, and me gone inside like whey the man name a Port Royal.

"Awright we going to town now in style," he concluded.

They all went back into the bus, resuming their seats and topics of conversation.

In a little while they began to pass the houses in the palatial residential heights of St. Andrew. Gussie looked up at them with longing and hope in his heart. He thought, "A hope a get a job with one a dem rich man; what a way them mus a rich, richer dan Mr. Ramsay, for fe him house no pretty like any a dese." He felt lighter hearing that Kingston was now a matter of minutes away. Perhaps Icilyn would still be waiting.

Gussie looked with amazement at the huge buildings they passed. When they reached the Parade his mouth gaped with unbelievable surprise and wonder. He saw the buses lined up on one side of the broad expanse of South Parade with another line of Kingston buses on the other side. People were everywhere. "What a heap of people," he thought.

The bus was unloading its human cargo, who once outside were busy clamouring for their baskets and other goods from the roof, all in a hurry to get away. No one paid Gussie any attention. He clutched his parcel under his arm and came off, stood by the side of the bus looking around, afraid to go far or to ask anyone a question. If Icilyn was coming she would have been there already, considering the bus should have come in at 2 o'clock and now it was 5 p.m. He was really dejected and nervous just standing there. Suddenly, he glimpsed Icilyn in the crowd. She was coming nearer to the bus and looking for him. "Thank God she come," he murmured to himself. He walked around and met her. "How do you do, Sister Icilyn, a glad you come you see, till a caan tell you; a tink you come already an gawn back."

"Mi know sey dem bus nevva on time, dem always late and me had tings finishing up a de yard. You see Kingston, bwoy. Dat's why me coulda nevva go back a country, me ha fi stay ya till me dead."

"Me no know if me gwine like it, it look big everlasting," Gussie replied.

"Cho, you wi' soon get fe know you way round. When me come ya, me nevva have a soul fe show me any way. One time a girl get a job fe me up a St. Andrew and me lass; mi nevva fine de place till slap inna de evening. When me go, the lady ask me whey happen to me, taut me was fe come from mawning. Mi tell her me nevva get the messige till late; me so shame, me couldn' tell her a lass mi lass."

They kept walking and talking for most of the way. Gussie looking on everything and every place with the eagerness of a child. Eventually they reached Icilyn's room which was in Jones Town. It was in one of those old tenement houses, which had seen better day. A group of children were playing in the yard. One called out, "Hi Miss Icy, you bredda come wid you?"

"Yes mi love," she answered and walked quickly past them to her apartment. Gussie was quite surprised to see her mahogany double bed, bureau, and china cabinet. She even had a washstand with basin and goblet. She saw the look of wonder on his face and said: "So you tink is fun me was mecking when me tell you bout me beroo an tings. Mi bwoy fren Tamatus nice to me caan done. Him help me buy all a dem. Dis town you can get by if you know how fe scuffle, but you haf fe work fe keep up a front. Come, you mus a hungry; me bring down nuff tings from whey me work. The lady me work wid, she no watch watch me, an she no like come ina di kitchen. She leave up everything to me. God bless whey she eat, everyday she say she pon diet, she no waan get fat, so me teck when the tecking is good. For some a dem employer dem mean so tell an hardly cook, dem only tink sey you can live pon breeze an still work hard. Anytime dem come wid dat, dem dont see me at all; is gone me gone."

Gussie listened, only grunting approval as he sucked the marrow from the pork bone which he was busily deciding to chew. He had eaten the four large dumplings and wiped the plate clean with a piece of breadfruit. She gave him a long drink of ginger beer.

His belly was full now. He twisted his neck and belched with deep satisfaction.

Icilyn looked on him and said, "You fit now, eh Guss?"

Later Icilyn made up a bed for Gussie in the corner of the room. She was hoping to get him a job where he could stop in, until he had saved enough money to get his own room. For the time being he was quite content to sleep on the floor. It was so clean and shining he could almost see his face in it. Everything was clean and tidy. No wonder Icilyn liked it here, the country was too heavy and muddy for her. He wondered, however, if he would ever get accustomed to it, the continual effort of keeping things in order, the closeness of the other tenants. He could hardly go far if they talked too much.

Icilyn had to leave early to go to work. She cautioned him, "Me know you awready how you selfish, but you mus talk now an den to di tenant dem in di yard, cause me and dem live nice.

Me dont run into dem, but me sey howdie to everybody, it no do no harm."

It was six weeks since Gussie arrived in Kingston, but up to now he had got no work. Everybody had tried, Icilyn had tried around where she worked, to no avail. He had even gone with Tamatus down to the wharf, but all the men belonged to the Union. They weren't taking on new hands, as the boats were mainly taking passengers and their baggage, but little cargo. Men were down there at the wharf waiting day after day, hope rising and dying with the sun, as the bananas were loaded on the ships. But you had to have the money to join the Union, and Gussie couldn't until he started working. Other men were there like him who just couldn't get a break, turning away disconsolately, hunger gnawing away at their vitals. "When they start shipping sugar you might get a break." That was what he had got to hold on to—the thin edge of hope. Until then, if he didn't have Icilyn he would die from starvation. What a life!

Everywhere you turned, things just didn't come out as you expected. You left the hard life in the country only to come and meet it a little worse in town. He was completely despondent. Six weeks of trying, of walking in search of work, until his toes in the crepe-soles stuck out like "ginger 'bove ground." Even Icilyn good humour and kindness were more than he could take these days. Once in a while she raved at him in anger, although she knew it was not his fault, for he was not lazy. He cleaned the room and did whatever he could find to do around the place.

He had walked the length and breadth of St. Andrew. When he knocked and asked respectfully for work, they looked on him with suspicion and anger for disturbing their enjoyment of leisure. He was determined that wherever and whatever it was, he would find employment before Tamatus rather than Icilyn became disgusted with him, openly resentful of his prolonged stay in Icilyn's room.

Icilyn had just come in. She was taking an assortment of things out of her grip. She poured some of the soup out of an Ovaltine tin into a cup for him, and from the different paper bags came rice and peas, chicken, beef and yam, already cooked. She shared out Tamatus' plate and covered it on the top of the cabinet. In a little while Gussie's plate was as clean as when it was bought. Icilyn looked on him and said, "Bwoy you did really hungry." Tama da tell me sey is time me get someting fe you fe do, Him know sey we all been trying fe help you, but it can hard eena di town; you know how it is wid man. Anyway you luck soon turn up, so no mine him. Is so life go sometimes, you only have fe try mek a start!

Gussie felt ashamed and sick from the bottom of his belly upwards. He wanted to get out and run, run far away from Icilyn, Tamatus, and everyone of the tenants in the yard; but his money had been finished weeks ago and if he left, where would he go? He had no one else to turn to in the big city. His mind was now made up. Tomorrow he would get a job or die in the attempt.

Up to late the next night Icilyn waited for Gussie to return to the room. She was worried, for he had never stayed out late; he had always returned sometime before her, if not a little after. The tenants had told her that he had left a few minutes after her that morning. Finally she decided he must have got work. Four days passed and still no word or sign of Gussie. She went to Sutton Street to enquire if he had got involved with the Law, while she begged Tamatus to go to the Hospital to see if he had met with an accident. Tamatus came back with nothing to tell.

He had gone through the Casualty Ward and the porter had looked through his list of names of those who were admitted for the past week, but Gussie's was not among them. When Tamatus saw how concerned Icilyn had become, he said: "Cho, no badda worry, the bwoy mus a fine some ooman fe mine him, or else him stow wey an gawn a Hinglan,"

Icilyn wailed, "No, Gussie wouldn't do dat; him too fraid fe trouble. When you gwine to work tomorrow, beg dem put it eena di papers sey him lass."

The women in the yard tried their best to comfort Icilyn, but she insisted that some untold disaster had overtaken Gussie. She tied her head with a bit of red cloth and sat in the middle of the yard and bawled: "Lawd, me one bredda gone now, him mus a drown himself a de sea. Lawd me no have no more fambily lef," she wailed.

Suddenly the zinc gate screeched open, the children in the yard were jumping and chattering, while the mongrels barked with half-starved persistency. When Icilyn turned her eyes in the direction of the hub-bub she saw Gussie coming in tattered and torn, holding a string of fish. Icilyn sat and waited until he came up to her. Gussie looked at her without a word. Icilyn had to break the silence, "Bwoy a whey you did dey, mek you go wey so long?"

Gussie sat down on the pile of stones where the women bleached their clothes, while the children and the tenants gathered around him. He said, "Lawd, if oonoo ever know all dat happen to me since a leave ya, a tink a dead done. Me go down a sea-side when a leave ya Monday morning. Me see some man pushing out a boat an a ask dem if me can come; dem no answer me, till one a dem say, 'Before you come help push out the boat'. So me get up an help dem. One a dem say, 'You fraid fè sea?

Me say, 'No sah, mi wi come."

"We have fe go far, far pass Port Royal, far out pass a heap a lickle islan' dem. Di sea rough, i' rough caan done; me frighten till me no know whey fe do. Mi vomit, mi sick, me sick everlastin; me cudun sick no more. When de wave dem come, dem higher dan de house. When dem a come over, me jus a pray to meself, 'Lawd, no mek mi drown for mi caan swim'. Dat was Monday night. After dat it calm down lickle and we trowout de net. De breeze start up back again and mi 'tink sey di boat was gwine bruk up. Di man dem start fe cuss and swear, some kine a bad word me nevva hear yet, how mi mus a de crossis dem pick up."

"More bad wud fly, and dem nearly trow me out a di boat. 'Di Boss-man him sey, "You know what, we betta lef dis bwoy out a de island dey an when we coming back we teck him up'. Me go pon di place an mi lay down an sleep ina di san'. When a wake up a hungry so till an all a coulda fine fi eat was some seaweed an sea-grape, but a eat till me mout taste stainy. Di breeze blow, rain come, an me bruk down some bush an bramble and meck up a little shelter. 'Den Wednesday mawnin eena di breeze-blow, a boat stop by di island an three man dem push it on di beach an teck shelter wid mi. Dem wasn't bad dough, dem gi me some food an water. Den di breeze stop blow eena di evenin, an di man dem ask me if me want go wid dem further on, because them was gwine fishin. Well a consider a little..."

"Icilyn could not wait, see queried, "Whey you sey to dem, bwoy?"

"Oh, me say awright, of course, for by dat time de fraid leave me an me sey if me coulda stan di breeze-blow an di other man dem, me caan do no worse; an a caan spen di rest a mi life out pon di islan."

"You heartful, dough, disaster mek you turn man same time," Icilyn rejoined.

"Well we push out back di boat. Dem have an engine pon it, an in no time we reach far out. Well sah, dem stop an put down di anchor and dem gi mi a line an mi bait it. A watch till di first man draw up him line an as a coulda let down mine eena di water a feel something tek hold a it an a hole tight an teck me time draw it up. See ya, when a use all me strength an bring it up, a nearly jump over di side of de boat, a see a snapper big an pretty like any mermaid. After dat, as fass as a put down de line a da draw up fish.

"Di man dem sey, 'Bwoy, you mus be a old time fisherman.'"

A sey, 'No sah, but it look like a going to be one from now an, for a like it.' A been gwine a di seaside everyday since a cudden get any wok fe do.

"Well de man dem say, 'You can get a job with us now for we go out three or four times a week. Meet we same place tomorrow evenin bout 4 o'clock." All the children and women cried, "Teng God, Gussie get work, teng God." Gussie picked up the string of fish he had brought along with him and handed it to Icilyn, and they walked up the steps to her room. When they reach inside, he shut the door and put his hand in his pocket and drew out two one-pound notes and said, "Icy teck dese, dat's what a get fi di big snapper."Icilyn's mouth opened, while her eyes showed only the whites, with astonishment. "Bwoy, you will do," she chuckled.

MARTIN LUTHER KING

In Peace he came
To spread Love
To his fellow man
Like the great
Aggrey of Africa
Knew
That the black keys
of the piano
Were as important
As the white
For both must play
The melody
Of the brotherhood of Man
He will not die in vain
Though strife and war
Prevail
For hearts will cry
And many heads will bow
In tribute
To another Martyr
Of Christian Unity and Love
"We shall overcome."

RT. HON. NORMAN MANLEY Q.C

We watched you through Life
Eloquent, dynamic and wise,
   True son of our soil,
   Rich in intellect, and strong, vibrant
   Destined to teach our people
Not to lead them...
now we weep because
   We did not
Give the love, the honour
and appreciation, you should
Have known.

Oh, we mourn, because our loss
   Is great and true.
Roll, then the drums forever,
   Though he be dead-
Yet lives deep in our hearts,
   Our tears of love cannot
   His buoyant figure rise
Or bring him back to earth:-
But we will build
A monument to him
The hero of our land,
Tried through the years,
   Now stilled by fate
   But not unsung.

OLGA MAE PASMORE

THE ROAD TO EMMAUS

Come, put your fingers
And touch the nails in his hands
And feel the emptiness beneath.
Come, put your hand into his side
And feel the gaping wound
Wherefrom the blood and water gushed.
Come, see the Tomb,
Where Jesus lay
And roll away,
The stone of unbelief-
The heavy burden of our thoughts,
And look into the Tomb,
The empty tomb where doubts
Have fled
And left the linen in its stead,
To teach us, as dear Thomas was,
That doubt can be an empty tomb
For Christ has risen from the dead
As he had said, He would,
And left instead
An angel guarding at the door
To walk with us to Emmaus
And lead us on the way
To truth and light and Life itself
Until another Day.

THE SAVIOUR OF THE WORLD

Hosanna, Hosanna,
They cried
Palms a waving
In exultation
He was acclaimed;
But with the Kiss of Judas
And thirty pieces of Silver
He was betrayed;
His deeds and miracles
        quickly forgotten...
The mad cry of the mob
Resounded...
"Crucify Him, Crucify Him!
Hanging from the cross
He forgave them all...
Came the glorious Easter Morn,
In the first light of dawn
They found
        The resurrected Christ
Fulfilling His prophecy,
Yet a little while, you shall not
                see me,
And again a little while
                Ye shall see me, because I go to the father
And no one comes to the Father
                But by me.

THE ROAD OF LIFE

There is no one who knows it all
This puzzling Road of Life
It has but too many turns and twists
For one to estimate its angles.
Its dimensions are so vast,
Its pot-holes big,
Its perspective wide
Its surface uneven
And its edges sharp and jagged
For it is the long, long road of Life
And one infinitesimal human being
Vainly tries to walk
With balanced steps.
Instead, gropingly tosses on his path
Holding in his hands, the dust and ashes
He has gathered to the end.

OLGA MAE

How I wish you were here,
So that I might put a shawl
Around your shoulders.
We often think old age is a must or a promise.
When you said to me at age thirty-five, "you are middle-aged,"
I was so annoyed
But you left us suddenly
A year less than your three score and ten.
        I miss you and feel your presence
From time to time.
You don't come as often as before
        But when the hummingbird visits I know it's you.
        With love forever and ever.

Tony Pasmore
25-MAY-2005

www.ingramcontent.com/pod-product-compliance
Lightning Source LLC
Chambersburg PA
CBHW041605240626
47164CB00008B/186